Note to parents, carers and teachers

Read it yourself is a series of modern stories, favourite characters and traditional tales written in a simple way for children who are learning to read. The books can be read independently or as part of a guided reading session.

Each book is carefully structured to include many high-frequency words vital for first reading. The sentences on each page are supported closely by pictures to help with understanding, and to offer lively details to talk about.

The books are graded into four levels that progressively introduce wider vocabulary and longer stories as a reader's ability and confidence grows.

Ideas for use

- Begin by looking through the book and talking about the pictures. Has your child heard this story before?

- Help your child with any words he does not know, either by helping him to sound them out or supplying them yourself.

- Developing readers can be concentrating so hard on the words that they sometimes don't fully grasp the meaning of what they're reading. Answering the puzzle questions on pages 30 and 31 will help with understanding.

For more information and advice on Read it yourself and book banding, visit **www.ladybird.com/readityourself**

Book Band 4

Level 1 is ideal for children who have received some initial reading instruction. Each story is told very simply, using a small number of frequently repeated words.

Special features:

Opening pages introduce key story words

woman

man

wife

clothes

boy

emperor

Careful match between story and pictures

One day a man came to see the Emperor.

"I can make you some beautiful new clothes," said the man.

Large, clear type

Educational Consultant: Geraldine Taylor
Book Banding Consultant: Kate Ruttle

A catalogue record for this book is available from the British Library

Published by Ladybird Books Ltd
80 Strand, London, WC2R 0RL
A Penguin Company

004

ISBN: 978-0-72327-276-2

Printed in China

The Emperor's New Clothes

Illustrated by Marina Le Ray

woman

man

boy

6

wife

clothes

emperor

One day, a man came to see the emperor.

"I can make you some beautiful new clothes," said the man.

The next day, the man came back.

"Do you like your beautiful new clothes?" he said. "Only clever people can see them."

"Yes," said the emperor.

But he could not see any new clothes.

The emperor saw his wife.

"Do you like my beautiful new clothes?" said the emperor. "Only clever people can see them."

"Yes," said his wife.

But she could not see the emperor's new clothes.

The emperor saw a man.

"Do you like my beautiful new clothes?" said the emperor. "Only clever people can see them."

"Yes," said the man.

But he could not see the emperor's new clothes.

The emperor saw a woman.

"Do you like my beautiful new clothes?" said the emperor. "Only clever people can see them."

"Yes," said the woman.

But she could not see the emperor's new clothes.

The emperor saw a little boy.

"Do you like my beautiful new clothes?" said the emperor. "Only clever people can see them."

"No," said the little boy.
"You do not have any
clothes on."

"Oh no!" said the
emperor and he ran
all the way home.

How much do you remember about the story of The Emperor's New Clothes? Answer these questions and find out!

- Who comes to see the emperor?

- What is special about the emperor's new clothes?

- What does the little boy say to the emperor?

Look at the pictures from the story and say the order they should go in.

 A

 B

 C

 D

Read it yourself with Ladybird

Tick the books you've read!

For children who are ready to take their first steps in reading.

Level 1

 The Enormous Turnip ☐

 Fairy Friends ☐

 Goldilocks and the Three Bears ☐

 Little Red Hen ☐

 The Magic Porridge Pot ☐

 Little Creatures ☐

 Recycling Fun! ☐

 The Princess and the Pea ☐

 Cinderella ☐

 Rex the Big Dinosaur ☐

 The Tale of Peter Rabbit ☐

 The Three Billy Goats Gruff ☐

 Why Giraffe has a Long Neck ☐

 Go to the Zoo ☐

 The Ugly Duckling ☐

 The Emperor's New Clothes ☐

For beginner readers who can read short, simple sentences with help.

Level 2

 Beauty and the Beast ☐

 Chicken Licken ☐

 Little Red Riding Hood ☐

 Nature Trail ☐

 Sports Day ☐

 Pirate School ☐

 Rumpelstiltskin ☐

 Sleeping Beauty ☐

 The Gingerbread Man ☐

 Sly Fox and Red Hen ☐

 The Tale of Jemima Puddle-Duck ☐

 The Three Little Pigs ☐

 Why Lion ROARRRS! ☐

 The Big Race ☐

 Town Mouse and Country Mouse ☐

 Dom's Dragon ☐

 Available on the App Store

The Read it yourself with Ladybird app is now available for iPad, iPhone and iPod touch

App also available on Android devices